P9-DCY-470

Peeping and Sleeping

by Fran Manushkin ★ Illustrated by Jennifer Plecas

WITHDRA
Property of
FAUQUIER COUNTY PUBLIC LIBRARY
11 Winchester Street
Warrenton, VA 22186

Clarion Books / *New York*

Clarion Books
a Houghton Mifflin Company imprint
215 Park Avenue South, New York, NY 10003
Text copyright © 1994 by Fran Manushkin
Illustrations copyright © 1994 by Jennifer Plecas

Illustrations executed in chalk pastel, oil pastel, and colored pencil on Canson paper
Text is 17/24 pt Novarese Book

All rights reserved.

For information about permission to reproduce selections from this book,
write to Permissions, Houghton Mifflin Company,
215 Park Avenue South, New York, NY 10003.

Printed in the U.S.A.

Library of Congress Cataloging-in-Publication Data

Manushkin, Fran.
Peeping and sleeping / by Fran Manushkin ; illustrated by Jennifer Plecas.
p. cm.
Summary: Barry and his father take an evening walk, investigating the strange peeping sounds they hear and finding a surprise down at the pond.
ISBN 0-395-64339-2
[1. Frogs—Fiction. 2. Night—Fiction. 3. Sound—Fiction.
4. Fathers and sons—Fiction.] I. Plecas, Jennifer, ill. II. Title.
PZ7.M3195Pd 1994
[E]—dc20 93-26297
CIP
AC

BVG 10 9 8 7 6 5 4 3 2 1

For Ursula Perrin—F.M.

For Nina—J.P.

Stars filled the sky
and peeps filled the night:
Peep-PEEP! *Peep*-PEEP! *Peep*-PEEP!

“Daddy, who’s that peeping?” Barry asked.
“I’ll show you,” said his father.
“Put on your slippers
and we’ll go outside.”

"Now? In the dark?"

"Yes, now." His father hugged him.

"I promise to stay nice and close."

So out the door
and down the path
the two of them walked,
holding hands in the warm spring night.

"Stay close," said Barry.
"I am," said his father.
As they walked down the hill,
the peeping grew louder:
Peep-PEEP! *Peep*-PEEP! *Peep*-PEEP!
And when they reached the pond,
the sound surrounded them:
Peep-PEEP! *Peep*-PEEP! *Peep*-PEEP!

"Here," said Barry's father,
"click this flashlight on,
and see what you can find."
"I'm a little scared,"
Barry whispered,
"but I still want to see."

Barry took a deep breath and counted, "One-two-three."
Then he turned on the flashlight: CLICK!
"All I see are weeds!" said Barry.

"Look harder," urged his father.

"I see frogs," Barry shouted. "Lots of tiny frogs!"

Peep-PEEP! *Peep*-PEEP! The frogs puffed into bubbles—
a bubble for every peep!

"So *you* are the peepers!"
Barry smiled.
"You guessed their name!" his father said.
"We call them spring peepers
because they pop out of the pond every spring."
"I guessed!" Barry said proudly,
and he flew his light around,
surprising peepers in the mud
and peepers in the weeds
and peepers swaying high in the breeze.
Peep-PEEP! *Peep*-PEEP! *Peep*-PEEP!

Barry watched the frogs hopping.
"Daddy, don't they ever sleep?"
"Not at night, maybe during the day."
"Daddy, I want to be a peeper!" Barry decided.
"Then *I* can stay up all night."
"Can you hop?" his father teased.
"You *know* I can," Barry answered,
and he hopped away, saying,
"Peep-PEEP! Peep-PEEP! Peep-PEEP!"

Then he shouted,
"Daddy, come be a peeper with me!"
"All right." And *he* leaped, too, saying,
"Beep-BEEP! Beep-BEEP!"
"Not *beep*." Barry giggled. "It's *peep*!"
"Right! PEEP-PEEP!" said his father.
And they hopped down the path.

"Whoops!"
Barry laughed.
"I hopped right out of my slippers."
His father stopped and got them.

"We peepers don't need to wear slippers,"
Barry decided.
"You're right," said his father,
and so they both hopped home barefoot
close as two frogs could be
through the long cool tickly grass.

"Here's *our* pond,"
pretended Barry
as they hopped into
the shimmering kitchen light.

"Now hop into bed,"
his father said.
Barry did,
and they said good night.

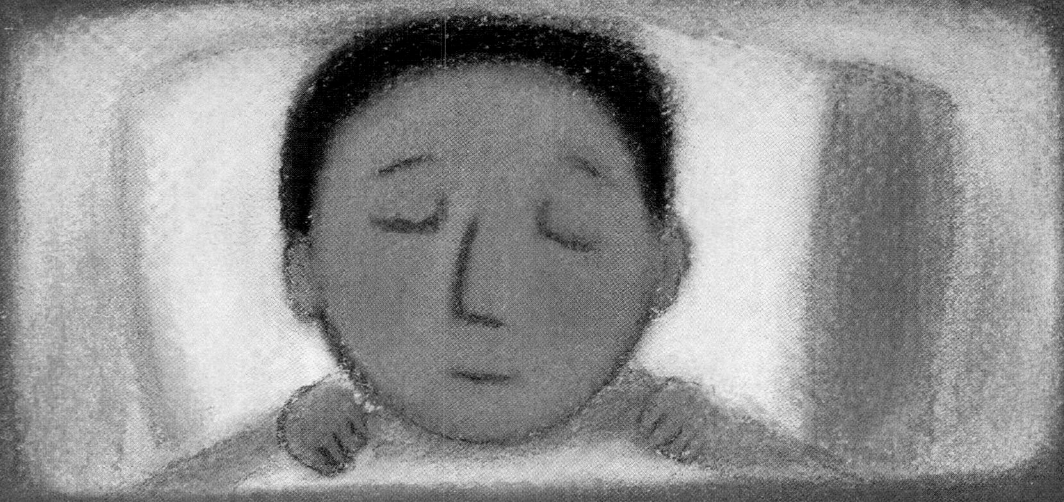

But as soon as Barry closed his eyes,
he heard a soft *Peep-Peep*! *Peep-Peep*!

Barry opened his eyes.
"There's a peeper in here!"

He looked around the room,
and then he swung upside-down
and peered under his bed.
"Daddy, come *quick*!" Barry called.
"There's a peeper in my slipper!"

"Stop teasing," his father said,
"and go to sleep."
"But it's true!" Barry insisted.
"Well, I'll *be*!" His father smiled.
"There *is* a peeper in your slipper.
He must have hopped inside
when your slippers came off."
"The peeper's lost," said Barry sadly.
"Let's take him back to the pond."

"He can find it himself," said Barry's father.
"Just put him on the windowsill
and watch what happens."
"Okay." Barry put the frog
in a puddle of moonlight.
"*Peep-Peep*?" the frog called.

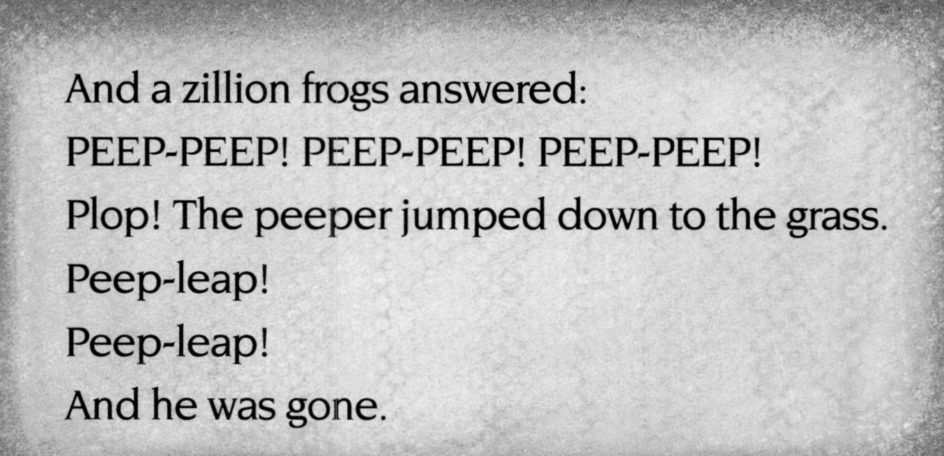

And a zillion frogs answered:
PEEP-PEEP! PEEP-PEEP! PEEP-PEEP!
Plop! The peeper jumped down to the grass.
Peep-leap!
Peep-leap!
And he was gone.

"Now it's back to bed," said Barry's father.
"Right!" said Barry.
"You won't hear another peep out of *me*."

And he closed his eyes,
and he softly crooned,
"Peep-sleep, peep-sleep, peep-sleep."
And as stars filled the sky
and frogs filled the pond,
Barry fell asleep,
asleep, asleep, asleep.